The big fish

Aoi Huber-Kono

Edizioni Corraini

Far   far away   on the sea,

there once was   a small
island
of fishermen.

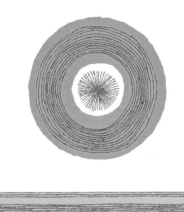

Every day
the big round sun
rose over   on the island.

On the sea   the waves

             chased rippling

                 towards infinity.

When

    the sun

        began

           to set

    the fishermen as usual went out to fish
        in their little boats, swaying

           on the high   sea.

By the time the sea breeze became stronger

and longer waves were sliding
across   the sea,

the boats reached   a place far away   from the island.

Darkness was falling
and all one could smell was
the dampness of the water.

One day while the fishermen,
were casting their nets,
all singing together,

a big unknown boat suddenly appeared
and seemed
to be looking in
their direction.

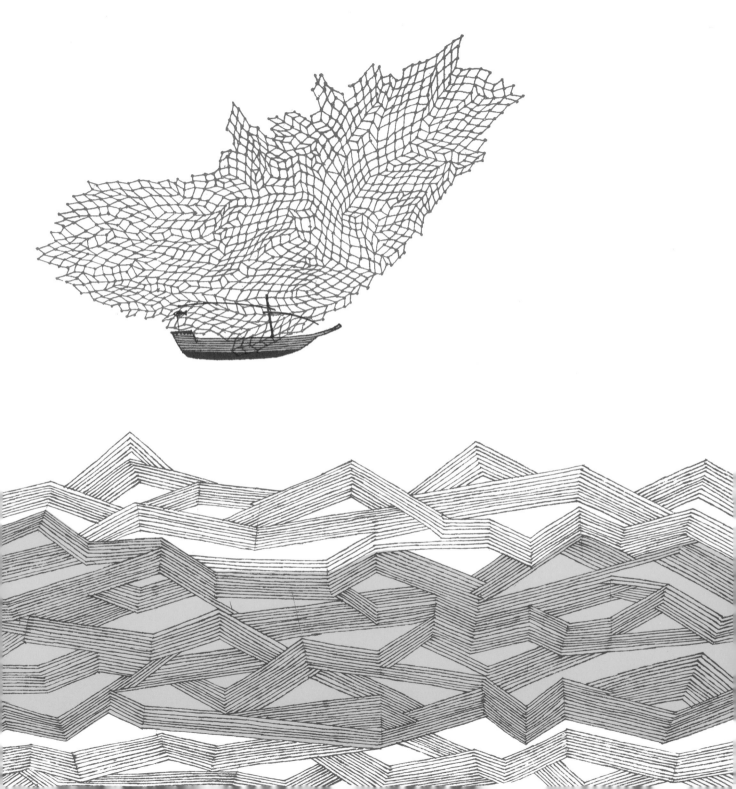

What was it?

The fishermen were very   surprized.

                    Until then nobody had ever seen
          such a strange thing.

Then from the belly of the big boat,
                          a door opened
                                    mysteriously,

                          a long net fell into the water
          and many, many fish
                          disappeared,

                          sucked
                          into
                          the
                          boat.

The next day too   this strange boat
                              appeared out at sea

                    and once again,
          started to fish
                    without ado.

And when the little boats drew near
                    to see what it was doing,

                    the big boat
                    hid itself on the bottom of the sea.

The fishermen
and all the inhabitants of the village   had no idea
                                                what to do.

As you can imagine,
even
if they put all the boats on the island together,
                    the mysterious boat would still be bigger than
                    they were.

                                        The fishermen could no longer
                                        fish:
                                        many had to
                                        give the boats
                                        back to their owners

Only the waves   came and went   on the shore
                                                as always,
                                        aware of nothing.

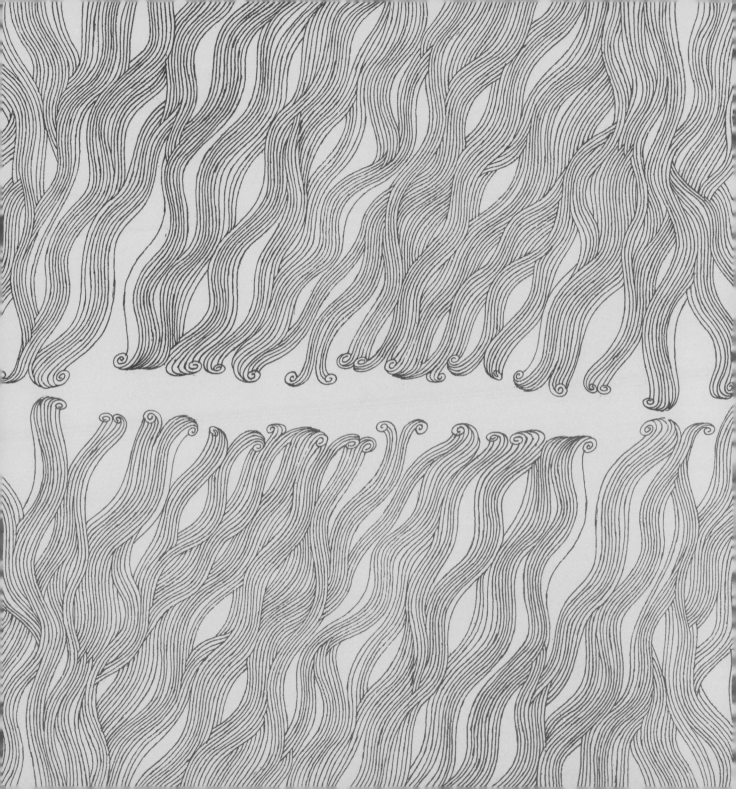

It happened
one evening at sunset.

Suddenly
the air
grew heavy   around the island,

                              the waves
                              started
                              to swell

          and a great storm approached.

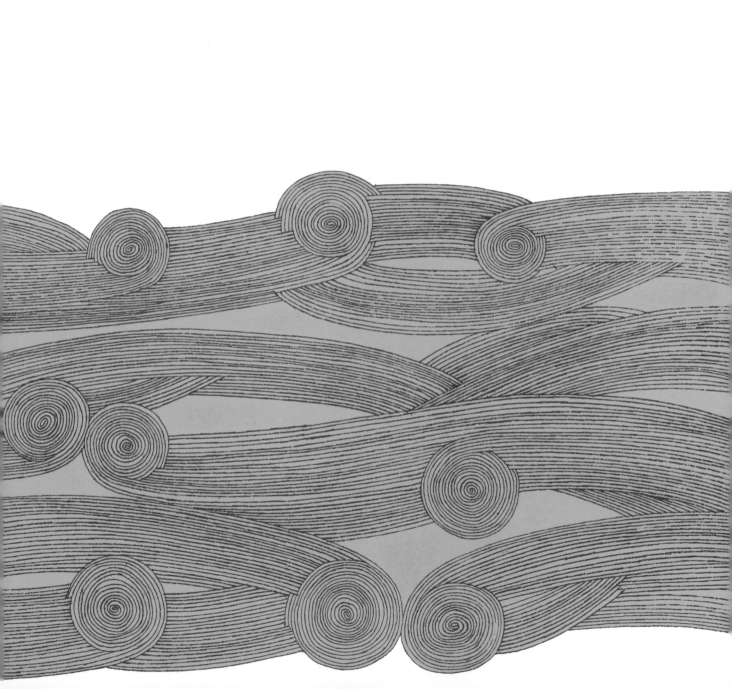

That evening,
              the waves
were so wild
              it seemed
                          they would
                          never stop,
              and the sea
                          was

so   fierce
                                      it seemed
                                      almost
              it wanted to
              swallow the island.

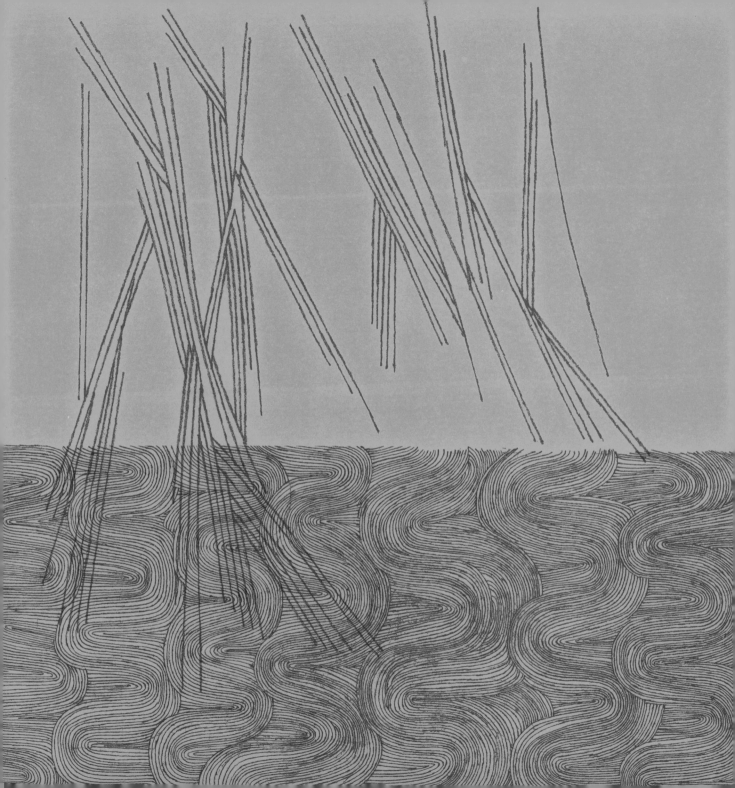

                    The lightning
glare wrapped
                    itself
        around
                    the island
        lit up
                    as if it were day.

Suddenly
for an instant one could see
on the lighted waters   a beautiful boat   passing by.

            But the violet light vanished at once

            and the sea
            began to make its threatening sounds again.

The inhabitants of the village
had never spoken to each other about the beautiful boat,

but they had began to think
it might be the sea lord of that island.

One fine morning,
six days later,

the waves   began

to glide   silently

across the shore again.

The storm was over.

The natives of the village
were finally reassured.

Everybody on the beach was happy.   Heave-ho...   heave-ho...
                                       Heave-ho...   heave-ho...
                                       Heave-ho...   heave-ho...

                                       the fishermen went to the village
                                       to show off
                        the big fish

                                       brought in by the storm.

Peace returned to the island.
Towards dusk
one could hear soft music in the air.

The big fish   had been thrown to shore by the waves.
It was a phantom fish,
all empty.

The strange boat had vanished,

swallowed by the storm.

That night
         the moon gently caressed   the village and the island

The sea,   majestic, kept silent.

Aoi Huber-Kono
The big fish
Original title of the work:
Il grande pesce

Original illustration and story by Aoi Huber-Kono
Original text layout by Max Huber, 1967
English layout edition by Arata Maruyama, 2006

First Corraini edition January 2007

Translated by Isobel Butters

Printed in Italy by
Grafiche SiZ, Verona
January 2007

Special thanks to Gabriele Capelli (publisher of the Italian edition)

Maurizio Corraini s.r.l.
via Ippolito Nievo, 7/A
46100 Mantova, Italy
T. +39 (0)37 632 27 56
F. +39 (0)37 636 55 66
E. sito@corraini.com
www.corraini.com